For Gwyneth, Margot, and Verity—and
all the other girls whose dreams are as
infinite as the universe—CH & EV

To Matt, for being my comrade in
exploration of this Universe—GR

PENGUIN WORKSHOP
An Imprint of Penguin Random House LLC, New York

Text copyright © 2021 by Catherine Hapka and Ellen Vandenberg.
Illustrations copyright © 2021 by Penguin Random House LLC.
All rights reserved. Published by Penguin Workshop, an imprint of
Penguin Random House LLC, New York. PENGUIN and
PENGUIN WORKSHOP are trademarks of Penguin Books Ltd, and the
W colophon is a registered trademark of Penguin Random House LLC.
Manufactured in China.

Visit us online at www.penguinrandomhouse.com.

Library of Congress Cataloging-in-Publication Data is available.

ISBN 9780593095713 (paperback)   10 9 8 7 6 5 4 3 2 1
ISBN 9780593095720 (library binding)   10 9 8 7 6 5 4 3 2 1

Astronaut Girl JOURNEY TO THE MOON

by Cathy Hapka and
Ellen Vandenberg
illustrated by Gillian Reid

Penguin Workshop

Chapter 1

SUMMER DAY SPLASHDOWN!

"Wake up, Astro Cat! Pay attention to the controls," I said. "We need to practice splashdowns."

Astro Cat yawned. He is a little lazy, but he's a pretty good first mate.

"Val," Mom called from across the yard. "Please watch the Baby—he's squashing my petunias."

Mom was working on some experiments in her garden. She's a botanist. That's a scientist who works with plants.

I am a scientist who works in space! Daddy is one of those, too. He is an astrophysicist. He was working at his lab today. And I was working at my lab. That's the gazebo in our backyard. Today I was pretending it was the Apollo 11 spacecraft.

"Sure, Mom," I said. "The Apollo 11 had a crew of three. The Baby can be part of the team."

Soon the three of us were in the spaceship. I double-checked my book, *The Universe*, to make sure I was getting everything right.

"Okay, let's focus, people," I told my crew. "A splashdown is how spaceships come back to Earth. A parachute helps them slow down as they fall through the atmosphere. Then they splash into the water to soften their landing."

Astro Cat yawned again, and the Baby was watching a butterfly. I wasn't sure they were paying close enough attention. But that was why I was the commander!

"We'll only have one chance to land back on Earth, so it's important to be prepared," I warned. I put on my helmet and set my stomp-on rocket launcher at the edge of the gazebo. "Begin the countdown, second mate!"

The Baby gurgled. He tossed a Cheerio out of the gazebo. That reminded me to put his helmet on, too. Astro Cat was sleeping, so I decided to let him be.

"Five!" I counted.

More Cheerios went flying.

"Four, three, two, one . . . liftoff!" I yelled.

I stomped on the launcher. The rocket flew toward Daddy's birdbath, ready to splashdown—and then right over it!

"Oh no!" I cried. "Malfunction! Malfunction! It went over the hedge!"

Suddenly the hedge started shaking. Then a face I'd never seen before poked through the leaves!

Chapter 2

MEETING WALLACE

"Hi," the face said. "I'm Wallace. We just moved in."

Then a hand appeared. It was holding my rocket.

"Is this yours?" Wallace asked.

"That's my rocket," I told him, grabbing it back.

Mom looked up. "Oh, hello," she greeted Wallace. "I heard we had new neighbors with an eight-year-old! Look, Val—a kid your age right next door! Come on over, Wallace. Welcome to the neighborhood!"

He came in through the gate. "Thanks," he told Mom. "My parents and Gramps and I just moved in, but we've been visiting for ages. My aunts and uncles and cousins all live here."

"How nice," Mom said with a smile. "That should make it a little easier getting settled."

"I hope so." Wallace smiled back at her. Then he looked at me. "Hi," he said. "Is that a spacesuit? I like it."

"Yes, it is," I said. "I made it myself."

"Cool," he said.

I noticed he was wearing a weird T-shirt. It said "Catch a Ride on a Comet."

"Why would you want to catch a ride on a comet?" I asked. "It's not like they go anywhere interesting. All they do is orbit the sun—just like Earth."

"How do you know that?" Wallace asked.

Mom chuckled. "Val knows everything about space," she said. "That's why we call her Astronaut Girl."

Wallace wandered toward the gazebo as Mom went back to work. "Wow!" he said. "That looks just like the alien rocket ship Commander Neutron used to breach a black hole in episode number sixty-three!"

Ugh! Now I knew where his T-shirt was from. "You watch *Comet Jumpers*, don't you?" I said. "That's a goofy show."

"It's not goofy, it's great!" he said. "It's my favorite show."

I rolled my eyes. If that was his favorite show, we probably wouldn't have anything else in common, either.

"I've seen *Comet Jumpers* a few times," I told him. "I wasn't impressed. The science is totally wrong."

Wallace shrugged. "The show is set in the year 3000," he said. "I'm sure science will be way more advanced by then. Use your imagination! It could happen."

I noticed the Baby trying to crawl down the gazebo steps. I picked him up before he could fall.

"Is that your brother?" Wallace asked.

"Uh-huh," I said. "He's my second mate. And that's Astro Cat over there. He's my first mate, but he's taking a break right now."

"Cool," Wallace said. "Just like Gloob is Commander Neutron's first mate."

"Yeah, but we're not the crew of some imaginary ship from a TV show," I said. "We're the crew of the Apollo 11 spacecraft."

"Apollo 11?" Wallace said. "I think I've heard of that . . ."

I couldn't believe my ears. Apollo 11 was only one of the most famous space missions in history! Daddy taught me all about it when I was still in diapers.

"I should hope you've heard of it!" I said. "The Apollo 11 mission was the first time humans set foot on the moon."

"Cool," he said. "Now I get why they call you Astronaut Girl."

"That's right," I said. "And did you know Apollo 11 almost never landed at all? There was a problem with the ship's computer, and Neil Armstrong had to take over and steer it himself. When they landed, there was only twenty-five seconds' worth of rocket fuel left, and—"

"Did you say rocket fuel?" Wallace interrupted. He pulled a battered notebook with a pencil stuck in the middle like a bookmark out of his pocket. "Cool term, I should use that in my story."

"What story?" I asked.

He explained that *Comet Jumpers* was running a contest for fans to send in story ideas. The best one would become a future episode.

"But I'm going to do better than that," Wallace said. "I'm going to write an entire script! I already have lots of notes and ideas. See?"

New Idea:

Zixtar activates the Beamatron with his hooked tail when the bad guys tie up his tentacles.

I read what he wrote. "Who's Zixtar?"
I asked.

He pulled something else out of his
pocket. It was an action figure.

"I made it myself," he said proudly. "This
is Zixtar. He's a new character I created for
my episode. He's an interstellar pirate!"

He held out the action figure, and I
grabbed it for a better look. It was actually

pretty cool. Zixtar
was made out of
polymer clay, like
the stuff I used
to make my
solar system
project for the
science fair. He
had five tentacles.
Each was a different

color and had a different tool on the end.

"What does the hook on his tail do?" I asked.

"That's for battling space monsters," Wallace said. "His tentacles have all kinds of powers."

I was a teensy bit impressed. Was Wallace really writing a TV script? Had he really created a whole new character?

Even so, I could tell he needed my help. "That's all cool," I said. "But there's no such thing as a Beamatron like on the show. You can't mush everyone's cells together into a giant ball of energy and then shoot them into space! They'd be lost forever. But there could be a way to move a spaceship full of people if it's stuck somewhere without power . . ."

"Oh yeah?" Wallace said, suddenly

interested. "What would do that?"

"Solar sails," I said with a grin.

"What's a solar sail?" Wallace asked.

"It's like a sailboat in space, but instead of wind, it uses solar power and mirrors to make ships move. See, you don't need a silly Beamatron! Just use solar sails instead. Think like a scientist!"

"Hmm, interesting," he said. "Solar sails could totally save the day when Commander Neutron's spaceship loses power while battling giant space bees . . ." He jotted down a few words. "Hey, if your idea makes it into the show, maybe the producers will put your name on-screen."

"They'd better," I said. "Because I'm your new cowriter!"

Chapter 3

THE PERFECT TEAM

"My cowriter?" Wallace said uncertainly.

"Of course!" I exclaimed. "You know the show, I know the science. We're the perfect team."

"Hmm," Wallace said. "I guess I could use some science help."

"Great," I said. "Let's start right now."

We decided to hold our first writers' meeting inside the Apollo 11 spacecraft. Wallace started heading toward the

commander's chair, but I beat him to it.
I grabbed my space pack off the second
mate's chair, since the Baby was playing
with some blocks on the floor and wasn't
sitting there anyway.

"You can sit here," I told Wallace.

Wallace sat down and opened his
notebook. "Here's what I have so far,"
he said. "Zixtar is battling to save the
endangered Cuddle Morphs."

"What's a Cuddle Morph?" I asked.

He smiled. "It's a new kind of alien. They
can transform into any creature as long
as it's furry." His smile faded a little. "My
friend Carlos from my old neighborhood
helped me come up with the idea."

He looked kind of sad all of a sudden.
I wasn't sure why. I decided not to mention
that morphing isn't as simple as he made

it sound. We could deal with that later.

"Okay," I said instead. "How does Zixtar save the Cuddle Morphs?"

Wallace perked up again. "He needs more weapons, so he goes to

the moon to collect the biggest Thunder Rocks he can find."

"Hold on a second," I said. "Are you talking about *Earth's* moon? Because there's no such thing as Thunder Rocks."

"Sure there are! They were on episode fourteen," Wallace said. "They explode when you throw them at stuff, with purple thunderbolts and a big BOOM!"

I shook my head. "You need my help even more than I thought," I said. "There's no thunder on the moon—in fact, there's no weather at all. Moon rocks are made of many of the same minerals we have on Earth. They don't explode!"

Wallace didn't look impressed. "How do you know?" he asked. "Have you been there?"

"No, but I know the science," I said.

Wallace grinned. "If you haven't been there, you don't know for sure that there's no such thing as Thunder Rocks," he said. "Anyway, this is just a TV show. Use your imagination!"

"Scientists use their imagination all the time," I said. "But that doesn't mean you have to make up stuff that doesn't exist."

"Whatever," Wallace said. "All I know is if I had a Beamatron here right now, I could beam up to the moon and find some Thunder Rocks."

I scowled. "You can't just BEAM UP to the moon!" I exclaimed. "Scientists and astronauts worked really hard for years to make space travel happen! If you think like a scientist, our script will be a lot better."

"Maybe, maybe not," Wallace said. "The Beamatron is really cool—you get in it, and then all your cells are scrambled and shot through a hole in space to get you where you're going."

"I already told you, that would never work!" I cried. "It's ridiculous! Anyway, the real story of space travel is way cooler than that kind of junk."

"Nothing's cooler than the Beamatron," Wallace argued. "Well, maybe Thunder Rocks are a little cooler . . ."

I couldn't take it anymore. "You know nothing!" I yelled. "I wish everyone had to go through basic astronaut training."

"I wish there really was such a thing as a Beamatron," Wallace said at the same time.

WHOOOSH! Suddenly the gazebo felt like it was tilting and spinning. Astro Cat squawked and hid under my space pack, and I heard the Baby gurgling happily. Everything went dark—except for a sky full of stars . . .

Chapter 4

LIFTOFF!

"What's happening?" Wallace cried.

I wasn't sure. But scientists love figuring out tough questions. "Let's collect the data," I said.

Everything stopped spinning. We weren't in the gazebo anymore.

"Where'd this weird little room come from?" Wallace sounded confused. "How did we get here?"

I looked around.

"It looks familiar in here," I said thoughtfully. There was a wall of computers in front of us with a window on each side. Astro Cat and the Baby were there, too.

Wallace's eyes looked really big. "Whoa!" he cried, pointing out the window. "Is that Earth?"

"Yes," I said. "I know exactly where we are. We're on the REAL Apollo 11 heading to the moon!"

"What?!" Wallace yelled. "That's amazing! How did we get here?"

"I don't know," I said with a grin. "But I've been training for this moment my whole life!"

"What do you mean?" Wallace asked.

"I'll be the commander," I said.

"Why do you get to be the commander?" Wallace argued.

"Because I'm Astronaut Girl, and Astronaut Girl always knows what to do!" I said.

He frowned but didn't say anything. So I looked around.

"Astro Cat, you're the capsule communicator," I decided.

"Communicator?" Wallace said. "He can't even talk!"

I ignored him. "The Baby can be lunar module pilot."

"Hey, if the Baby gets an important job, I should have one, too!" Wallace said.

"Fine. You can be the command module pilot," I told him.

"What's a command module?" he asked.

I explained that Apollo 11 was made up of three separate spacecraft, called modules. We were in the command module, which was called *Columbia*. That was where the astronauts lived and worked. The service module contained the rocket engine and storage space. The lunar module was called *Eagle*. That was the part that landed on the moon.

As I talked, Wallace started floating around. It was distracting.

"Hold still," I told him.

"No way, this is fun!" Wallace grinned and did a flip in the air. "I'm weightless!"

The Baby was floating, too. He giggled and tried to grab Zixtar as he floated past. I looked at Astro Cat. He was the only one being sensible. He was using his claws to hang on to the commander's chair.

"It's called zero gravity," I said.

Wallace wasn't listening. He did three backflips in a row.

"Being weightless makes me thirsty,"
he said. He pulled a juice box out of his
pocket.

"No!" I cried.

Too late. Droplets of grape juice flew
everywhere.

The Baby opened his mouth and tried to
swallow a few droplets, but his helmet got
in the way.

"Way to go, Baby. That's a good idea!" Wallace chased down the rest of the juice droplets. "Mmm, drinking in space is much more exciting than on Earth!"

I sighed. "That's why you can't bring regular food and drink to space," I said. "Otherwise there would be crumbs floating around everywhere. All food has to be freeze-dried or thermo-stabilized—"

"Thermo what?" Wallace asked.

"It's like canning food, except in a pouch instead of a can," I explained. "Luckily, I always keep space food in my pack."

I passed out pouches of astronaut food. Wallace made a face when he saw his.

"Yuck, I don't like broccoli," he complained. He swapped with the Baby, who had macaroni and cheese.

Astro Cat gobbled his tuna casserole
before I could even add water to it. I tasted
the lasagna. It was kind of gross, but I
didn't say so. I wished I hadn't already
eaten all the ice-cream packets.

While everyone was eating, I said, "It's time to discuss what happens next."

"What do you mean?" Wallace asked with his mouth full.

"We have to be ready to land on the moon," I said. "That means we have to be in *Eagle*. I already told you, that's the lunar module."

"Wait, is that why people say 'The *Eagle* has landed'?" Wallace exclaimed. "Cool! But what happens to the other two modules?"

I sighed, trying to stay patient. Daddy always says that not everyone knows as much about space as we do.

Then I explained how it worked again.

"*Columbia* and the service module will stay in orbit while we're on the moon," I said. "I'll write a computer code so it can do that without a person at the controls. Then we'll fly *Eagle* back up to join with the other two modules again."

"Wow, so we're really going to walk on the moon?" Wallace said.

I picked up my helmet. Astro Cat and the Baby still had theirs, too. But Wallace was only wearing his shorts and T-shirt.

"You can't walk on the moon without a helmet and space suit," I told him. "You need the helmet to breathe because there's no oxygen on the moon. And the suit protects you from the extreme cold of space and the sun's radiation."

The Baby was still floating around chasing one last juice droplet. He bounced off a cabinet door and giggled. The door opened.

"Hey, look!" Wallace said. "There are

helmets and space
suits in here."

We found
one that fit
him. There
was even a
tiny helmet
for Zixtar!

"Okay, we're
almost ready,"
I said. It took
a few seconds
to figure out how to work the computer—
it was really old-fashioned. But writing
the code was easy. After all, I won Best
Junior Coder at tech camp.

When I was finished, we climbed into
Eagle.

"Strap in for lunar landing!" I ordered.

"Monitor speed and altitude, Astro Cat. I'll fire up the steering rockets. Moon, here we come!"

Chapter 5

ON THE MOON

"The *Eagle* has landed!" I cried as the lunar module touched down. "Time to explore!"

We climbed down the ladder out of *Eagle* and stepped onto the moon. The sky was black, and the stars were really bright.

Wallace's eyes were huge inside his helmet. "Wow," he said. His voice sounded weird over the radio in my helmet. "It looks like a desert at night."

"That's because there's no atmosphere on the moon," I told him. "There are no clouds, no weather, and no air. So when you look up, you're staring straight into outer space. No air also means plants and animals can't survive here."

Astro Cat seemed worried. I gave him a pat. He would be fine in his helmet!

Wallace took a step. He bounced up in the air.

"Whoa, walking is different on the moon!" he exclaimed. "It feels like I could jump over a house!"

I tried it, too. "Look, Astro Cat!" I said. "I can finally do a backflip!"

The Baby looked excited. He flapped his arms—and bounced right over Astro Cat!

"I guess there's no gravity here, either," Wallace said.

"Actually, there is," I explained. "It's just less than on Earth, because the moon is much smaller. So its gravitational force isn't as strong."

Wallace nodded. He was having too much fun to ask any more questions.

I looked around. "We landed in the right place," I told the others. "This is the Sea of Tranquility."

"Too bad we didn't bring surfboards,"

Wallace said with a grin.

"It's not that kind of sea," I told him. "The craters on the moon are called seas because early astronomers thought the dark patches they saw through their telescopes were filled with water. But there's no water on the moon's surface, only underground."

"I was just kidding," Wallace said. "But wouldn't it be cool to surf on the moon? Maybe we should add that to our script!"

I decided to ignore that. "Anyway, this is where the Apollo 11 astronauts landed," I said. "Let's look for the stuff they left behind."

"What kind of stuff?" Wallace asked.

I spotted something white in the distance. It only took a few big leaps to reach it. "This must be the American flag," I said.

"What?" Wallace exclaimed. "That's not the American flag! It's white!"

"That's because it faded. The sun's rays are really strong here because there's no atmosphere. Plus it gets really hot and really cold, so stuff wears out faster."

"Wow," Wallace said. "In school, we learned not to let the American flag touch the ground. We should stand it up."

"Okay," I said.

Together, we picked up the flag. We stuck it in the ground.

"Much better," Wallace said. He pointed. "What's that?"

Something shiny was gleaming in the distance. We bounced over to take a look.

"I know what this is!" I said. "The Apollo 11 astronauts left it here on purpose. It's called the Lunar Laser Ranging Retroreflector. It's their only science experiment that's still running. It reflects lasers from Earth to measure the distance between Earth and the moon. That helps scientists learn about stuff like gravity and the moon's orbit."

I explained more about how it all worked. After a moment, Wallace started making notes. I was glad to see that he was finally taking science seriously!

New idea!

Add laser mirror to Zixtar's armor for combating laser-eyed aliens!

There were lots of boot prints nearby. It was cool to think that Neil Armstrong and Buzz Aldrin had left them.

And now my footprints would be here, too!

"One small step for a girl, one giant leap for girlkind," I declared.

"Girlkind?" Wallace said. "What about boykind? And alienkind—Zixtar can leave a tentacle print!"

"Don't forget catkind," I said, pointing to Astro Cat. I grabbed the Baby before he could bounce off again. "And babykind, too."

Wallace looked distracted. "Hey, I want to see the Julius Caesar crater. Do you know where it is?"

"How do you know about the Julius Caesar crater?" I asked in surprise. "I thought you didn't know anything about the moon."

"Everyone knows about the Julius Caesar crater," he said. "That's where Thunder Rocks come from!"

"I told you! There's no such thing as Thunder Rocks!" I exclaimed. "There is a real Julius Caesar crater, though."

"Cool! Let's go there," Wallace said.

"There are no Thunder Rocks," I told him. "But we can go there if you want. I'd like to collect some moon rock samples from different spots." I strapped the Baby to my back and grabbed my space pack. "Let's go!"

Chapter 6

SEARCHING FOR ~~THUNDER~~ MOON ROCKS!

I pulled *The Universe* out of my pack to check the location. "The Julius Caesar crater is due west of the Sea of Tranquility," I said.

"Okay," Wallace said. "Which way is west?"

I reached into my pack for a compass. Then I remembered something.

"The magnetic field on the moon is a lot weaker than Earth's," I said. "That means compasses don't work here."

"Oh, okay," Wallace said. "Well, all we need to know is which way west is, right?"

"Yes," I said. "Now be quiet, I'm thinking."

"Don't tell me to be quiet," he said, sounding annoyed. "You sound like my cousins."

"Are your cousins scientists like me?" I asked, suddenly interested.

"No, they're just older and think they know everything." He stared up at the sky and pointed. "Anyway, there's Orion's Belt."

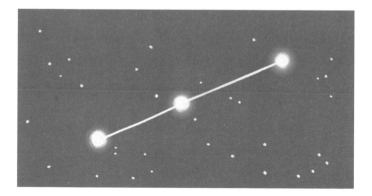

"That's what regular people call it," I said. "Those three stars are really called Alnitak, Alnilam, and Mintaka."

"It doesn't matter what name you use," he said. "It means that way is west."

I realized what he was saying. "You're right *and* wrong," I said. "On Earth, that would be west. But here on the moon we're seeing the constellation from a slightly different angle, which means . . ."

I did some quick calculations in my head. "*That* way is west!"

"Lead the way due west, Zixtar!" Wallace sang out, wiggling his action figure.

Astro Cat and I followed them. "How did you know that stuff about finding your way with the stars?" I asked Wallace.

"My gramps was in the Coast Guard," he said. "He taught me all the constellations and how to use them to find my way."

"Interesting," I said. "Did you ever get lost and have to use it?"

He didn't answer for a second. He was a little ahead of me.

"Are you listening?" I said. "Is your radio working?"

"Yeah, yeah," he replied. "But I think I just spotted a Thunder Rock up there! What do you think, Zixtar?"

I rolled my eyes. "We're not even to the Julius Caesar crater yet," I said. "Besides, I keep telling you there's no such thing as Thunder Rocks!"

"I don't know, there are tons of rocks around here." Wallace waved his arm. "Who says none of them are Thunder Rocks?"

"I do," I said. "That one right there is volcanic. That other one is called a mare basalt, and it's similar to some rocks on Earth ..."

I kept telling him about moon rocks until we reached the edge of the Julius Caesar crater. It was a lot deeper and rockier than the Sea of Tranquility.

"Wow, this crater is huge!" Wallace exclaimed. "There definitely could be Thunder Rocks here somewhere."

I didn't bother to respond. Instead, I pulled my shovel, sample bags, and tongs out of my pack.

"What are those for?" Wallace asked.

"I need to collect as many samples of moon rocks and dirt as I can," I said. "Three new minerals have been discovered on the moon so far. Maybe I'll discover a fourth one! Maybe they'll even name it

after me, like they named one after the Apollo 11 astronauts!"

"They did?" Wallace said.

I nodded. "It's called armalcolite," I said. "The *arm* is for Armstrong, the *al* is for Aldrin, and the *col* is for Collins."

"Cool," Wallace said. "We can call our mineral walvalite."

"Don't you mean valwalite?"
I corrected him.

"No, I mean walvalite," he said. "That sounds way better."

"Who cares how it sounds," I said. "My name should come first."

Wallace put his hands on his hips. "Says who?"

"Me—and I'm the commander, remember?" I said. "Good thing, too, or this whole mission would be about

54

finding Thunder Rocks that don't even exist."

"You may think you know everything about everything, but you don't!" Wallace said. "Come on, Zixtar. Let's go explore by ourselves for a while."

He stomped off. Astro Cat wandered after him.

"I never said I know everything about everything," I answered. "Wallace? Can you hear me?"

There was no reply over the radio. I wasn't sure what to do. Why was Wallace acting so weird all of a sudden? My friends Molly and Ling sometimes laughed and called me Professor Val when I talked too much about space. But they never got mad about it.

"Let's get back to work," I told the Baby. "That always makes me feel better."

Just then an interesting moon rock caught my eye. I bounced over to it.

"I think this is a lunar breccia!" I exclaimed. "Those are rocks created by the impact of a meteor."

There were lots of interesting samples here. I was careful to seal them all in my sterile sample bags. I didn't want to bring the moon flu back to Earth!

Finally my bags were all full. "Okay, let's move on," I said.

Nobody answered. I looked around.

"Wallace?" I said. "Astro Cat? Where did they go?"

The Baby gurgled.

"Wallace?" I said again, louder. "Do you copy? Answer me!"

"I'm still looking for Thunder Rocks," Wallace finally answered. His voice sounded staticky. "I walked pretty far. I'm not sure where I am."

"I can't see you!" I said. "Which direction did you walk?"

"I think it was—"

The static covered his voice. Then there was a click, and the radio went dead!

I gulped. "Houston, we have a problem . . ."

Chapter 7

LOST ON THE MOON!

"Wallace!" I shouted. "Astro Cat!"

I bounded toward the last place I'd seen them. They had to be around here somewhere!

I yelled their names over and over. But the radios still weren't working.

The Baby squirmed. "It's okay," I told him. "We'll find them."

But when I looked around, it was hard to tell which direction to go. Everything was

gray and dusty and looked the same.

"Maybe they went back to *Eagle*," I said. "We'll meet them there."

That's when it hit me. I wasn't sure how to find my way back!

If only my compass worked here, there would be no problem. But it didn't. If only I'd invented a special moon-tracker app at tech camp. But I hadn't.

What was I going to do?

DAY 1, HOUR 1: Zixtar
and I are lost, with only
a cat for companionship.
The cat is calm, but I am
worried. How will I find the
others? Will I be stuck here
forever, living in a crater
and eating moon rocks?

Maybe it's better this
way. Maybe I won't miss
Carlos and the others
from back home as much
up here. And I'll never
have to be the new kid at

school. Or have to sit by myself at lunch.

But if I stay here, it means I'll never see the blue skies of Earth again. Or kick the winning goal for my soccer team. Or help Mom make mashed potatoes for Sunday dinner at Aunt Celia's.

No, I definitely have to go back! Gramps keeps telling me I'm going to love my new hometown. And maybe he's right. I already have one new friend. Now all I have to do is find her . . .

I wish more than ever that Comet Jumpers was real. That way I could just hop into the Beamatron and go home. Or at least call a Snargle beast, like the one in episode 30 that guided Commander Neutron back to his ship . . .

"No need to worry, Baby," I said. "I'm Astronaut Girl, and Astronaut Girl never gives up."

I sat down on a large mare basalt to think. There had to be a way to find *Eagle*.

But even if I did find it, what about Wallace and Astro Cat? Wallace wasn't very good at thinking like a scientist. He would probably just try to pretend the Beamatron was real.

Or would he? I remembered how his gramps taught him to use the stars to navigate.

"That gives me an idea," I said to the Baby. "On some of the Apollo missions, the astronauts had to use an old sailor's tool called a sextant to guide them. I think there's a chapter in *The Universe* that could show me how to build one ..."

DAY 1, HOUR 1.5: I'm still dreaming about the Beamatron being real.

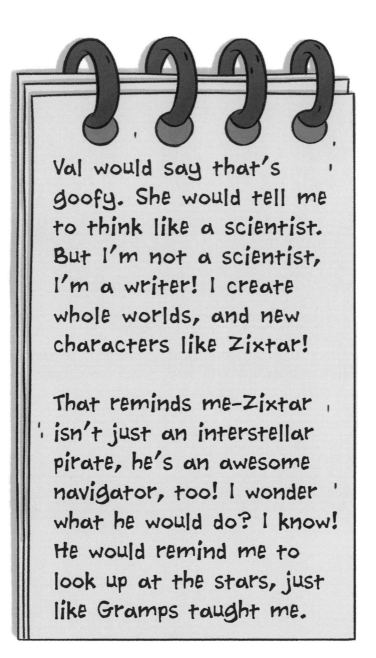

Val would say that's goofy. She would tell me to think like a scientist. But I'm not a scientist, I'm a writer! I create whole worlds, and new characters like Zixtar!

That reminds me-Zixtar isn't just an interstellar pirate, he's an awesome navigator, too! I wonder what he would do? I know! He would remind me to look up at the stars, just like Gramps taught me.

Actually, I bet Val would say that, too.

We came west to get here. Now all I have to do is use the stars to figure out which way is due east . . .

Chapter 8

NEW IDEAS

Just as I'd thought, *The Universe* had instructions for making a sextant. I had all the materials in my pack—ruler, protractor, tape, string, and paper clips. It pays to be prepared!

Back on Earth, making the sextant would have been super easy. It was a little harder on the moon, since I was wearing bulky space gloves. But I did it! Then I used my homemade sextant to figure out which way I needed to go to find *Eagle*.

"It's this way, Baby," I said. "Watch for anything familiar."

I'd been walking for a while when there was a loud squawk from the radio. A second later, I heard Wallace's voice. He was singing the theme song from *Comet Jumpers*.

"Hey, Command Module Pilot!" I said. "I think the radios are working again!"

"Ahoy there, Commander!" Wallace exclaimed. "Where are you? I think I just spotted *Eagle* up ahead."

"I can't see it yet, but the Baby and I are on our way," I said. "Is Astro Cat with you?"

"Yes, and Zixtar, too," he replied.

"How did you get back so fast?" I asked.

"I used the stars to navigate," Wallace

said. He told me all about it while I kept walking. A few minutes later, I finally saw *Eagle* sticking up from the Sea of Tranquility. Wallace and Astro Cat came rushing to greet me.

"We found it!" I cried, leaping forward. I grabbed Astro Cat and hugged him. He didn't try to wiggle away for once. I guessed he was as glad to see me as I was to see him.

I was kind of glad to see Wallace, too. "I was afraid you might be lost on the moon forever," I told him.

"Why would you think that?" Wallace said. "I'm the one who figured out how to get to the crater in the first place."

"You're right," I said. "It's cool that you know how to navigate with the stars."

"I was a little worried when the radio cut

out," Wallace admitted. "But it was almost like I could still hear you saying 'think like a scientist.' That reminded me that I knew how to find my way back. I even remembered to adjust for being on the moon, like you told me."

"That's so funny," I said. "The same thing happened to me! I remembered you talking about your gramps, and that made me think

about how sailors used to navigate, and that reminded me of something called a sextant. You know, we really do make a pretty good team."

Wallace smiled.

"Are you tired?" he asked. "I could take the Baby for a while if you want."

"Sure, thanks." I unstrapped the Baby and handed him over. Wallace stuck Zixtar in the pocket of his space suit, then strapped the Baby onto his back.

"So, what's a sextant? That sounds familiar," Wallace asked.

"Your gramps probably knows how to use one," I said. "Here, I'll show you how I made it."

I pulled out *The Universe* and opened to the right page. Wallace leaned closer.

Just then the Baby gurgled. "Hey, stop pinching me," Wallace told him with a laugh.

We looked at the book together, and I showed him the sextant I'd built.
I explained that a sextant measures the

angle between two objects. By adding some math, you can figure out which direction to go, whether you're sailing a ship on the sea or you're walking on the moon.

"Cool!" Wallace said when I finished explaining all that. "A sextant sounds like something Zixtar could use to navigate."

"That's a good idea," I agreed. "Then he could still find his way even if there's no power."

Wallace nodded. "I bet I could build it onto the end of a tentacle. Maybe the one next to the one with the lightning rod . . ."

"Wait, which tentacle is that?" I asked.

"I'll show you." He reached into his pocket and felt around. Then he frowned. "Didn't I put him in here?"

He checked all his other pockets.

"Where is he?" I asked.

"Oh no!" Wallace cried. "Zixtar is gone!"

Chapter 9

GOING HOME

Wallace spun around, staring in all directions.

"Don't worry, we'll find Zixtar," I said. But I wasn't sure that was true. The moon was huge!

"We have to retrace our steps," Wallace cried. "I must have dropped him on the way back from the crater."

Then I thought of something. "No, you didn't," I said. "I saw you put him in your pocket just now. He has to be nearby."

I thought that would make him feel better. But Wallace's eyes were still wide and anxious. "We have to find him!" he insisted. "I'm not leaving without Zixtar!"

I was a little surprised. He sounded really upset.

"It's okay," I said. "He's just an action figure."

"Just an action figure!" Wallace shouted. "He's more than that to me! I spent tons of time making him and figuring out all his powers and—"

"No, wait!" I broke in. "I didn't mean it that way. I just meant he can't walk off on his own. If we stay calm and think logically, we'll find him."

Wallace still looked worried, but he nodded. "I guess you're right," he said. "You look that way, and I'll check this way."

We started searching. It should have been easy to spot Zixtar, since he was so colorful. But there was no sign of him.

"I don't see him anywhere," Wallace moaned. "Oh, Zixtar, where could you be? I need to get you back so we can add that sextant to your tentacle!"

Just then the Baby gurgled and flapped his arms. He had something in one hand.

"Zixtar!" I exclaimed. "Look, Wallace, the Baby must have grabbed him out of your pocket."

"Zixtar!" Wallace pried the action figure out of the Baby's hand. "Whew, I'm so glad to see you!"

I was afraid the Baby might cry when Wallace took Zixtar away. He did that sometimes when I made him stop drooling on my telescope. But he just yawned instead.

"Looks like it's almost naptime," I said. "We should get the Baby home before he needs his diaper changed."

Wallace nodded. "Visiting the moon has been wild," he said. "But I'm getting hungry. Let's go home."

Zixtar in hand, he led the way toward *Eagle*. Then he paused, staring at something on the ladder. "Hey, what's that?" he said.

I looked where he was pointing. "Oh, I almost forgot about that," I said. "It's a plaque the Apollo 11 astronauts left here."

"Cool," Wallace said. "Let's sign our names, too."

We scratched our names on the ground beneath the plaque. I signed for the Baby, and Wallace helped Zixtar make a big *Z*. Astro Cat left his paw print.

"Okay, let's go," I said. "Earth, here we come!"

We climbed into *Eagle* and strapped in. I grabbed the controls.

"Prepare for liftoff!" I cried.

Eagle rose into orbit around the moon. A few minutes later we spotted *Columbia* and the service module. The computer took over steering and joined all three modules together again.

"Everyone, get back to *Columbia*," I said. "Next stop, Earth!"

Once we were all in *Columbia,* I released *Eagle* from the other two modules. Then I started up the rocket engine, and we headed toward home. It was a smooth ride until after we released the service module and entered Earth's atmosphere.

"Fire up the thrusters, Astro Cat," I said. "We need to make sure the module is in the right position. Gravity will do the rest. But hold on, it's going to be a bumpy ride!"

"You aren't kidding about that!" Wallace yelled, holding on for dear life as *Columbia* rattled and shook. "Whoa, I think gravity just came back!"

"Yeah," I said. "I feel like I weigh more than Daddy!"

"I weigh more than an elephant!" Wallace exclaimed.

I laughed. "I weigh more than the Empire State Building!"

I looked out the window. We were almost there. I knew what to do.

"Release the drogue parachutes, Command Module Pilot!" I said.

Wallace looked confused. "What are those?"

I did it myself. "They're the special parachutes that slow us down for splashdown," I explained. "Brace yourselves—we're almost there!"

I looked out the window one more time. The ocean looked like it was speeding toward us. I closed my eyes and prepared for impact.

Chapter 10

DOWN TO EARTH

I opened my eyes. We were all back in the gazebo. Astro Cat was clinging to me with all his claws. I peeled him off.

"We made it," I exclaimed, flinging off my space helmet.

Mom looked up from her plants. "Everything okay over there, kids?" she called.

"Better than okay!" I replied. "We just got back from the moon!"

"It was really cool," Wallace added. "Zixtar loved it!"

"Who's Zixtar?" Mom asked.

"Wallace invented him," I told her. "He's this really cool alien pirate."

Mom chuckled. "I'm surprised you all came back so soon."

I carried the Baby over to her. "We came back because he needs his diaper changed," I said.

Mom headed into the house with the Baby. When I got back to the gazebo, Wallace was scribbling in his notebook.

"I have lots of ideas for our script," he said. "Maybe Zixtar gets lost in a black hole and has to use his tentacle sextant to escape."

"I don't think a sextant would work in a black hole," I corrected him.

Wallace scowled. Then he smiled. "Okay, then what if he gets lost in the asteroid belt instead?"

I thought about that. "Sure, that could work."

"Cool!" Wallace wrote it down.

Just then we heard someone calling his name. An older man peered over the hedge and waved. "There you are, Wallace," he said. "It's time for lunch."

"Coming, Gramps," Wallace said.

He looked at me. "Can we have another writers' meeting after lunch?"

"Sure," I said. "I'll see you then."

Notes for script:

1. Low gravity on the moon means Zixtar can do a backflip during a fight scene!

2. Have bad guys scramble the stars so Zixtar can't navigate- but he can still use his sextant tentacle!

3. Use Thunder Rocks to destroy the star- scrambling ray!

Notes from cowriter/chief science adviser: There's no way someone could scramble the stars. And THERE'S NO SUCH THING AS THUNDER ROCKS!!!!!!!!

BLAST OFF ON EVEN MORE ADVENTURES WITH ASTRONAUT GIRL!